Trick Arrr Treat

A PIRATE HALLOWEEN

LESLIE KIMMELMAN

pictures by
JORGE MONLONGO

Albert Whitman & Company
Chicago, Illinois

The pirate chief's mom calls a meeting.

"Ready for some trick or treating?
Be home by dark, and watch the sun—
when it goes down, this gang is done."

The pirate chief slams shut the door
and then announces, "One rule more.
Don't you smile and don't be sweet.

Scowl and holler,

'TRICK ARRR TREAT!'"

"I be brave!" says Glass-Eyed Gabby.

"I be bold!" says Peg-Leg Pete.

"I be fierce!" says Toothless Tim.

"And we be pirates. TRICK ARRR TREAT!"

Pirates down the dark streets creeping.
Pirates lunging, pirates leaping.

Pirates stomping, pirates clomping.
Pirates house to house a-romping.

"Give me loot,"
says Charlotte Blue-Tongue.

"Pieces of eight," says Rude Ranjeet.
"Treasure," orders Dreadful Davey.

"We be pirates.
TRICK ARRR TREAT!"

Pirates sticking out their tongues,
shrieking with their pirate lungs.

Pirates cheering, pirates jeering,
pirates everyone be fearing.

Then the noise of panting, slurping.
"What be that?" asks Peg-Leg, burping.

Rude Ranjeet can only shrug,
gives his pirate mates a tug.

Pirates sneaking door to door.

Pirates peeking, wanting more.

Pirate plunder overflowing.
Happy pirates yo-ho-ho-ing!

"Fill my belly!" says Charlotte Blue-Tongue.

"Rot my teeth!" says Rude Ranjeet.

"Shiver me timbers!"
says Glass-Eyed Gabby.

"We be pirates. TRICK ARRR TREAT!"

Scary shadow pirates spy.
What Halloween horror lurks nearby?

A sea serpent that wants to fight?
Fearsome pirates shake with fright!

Toothless Tim gasps, "Go away."

Dreadful Davey yells, "Yeah, scram!"

Charlotte Blue-Tongue adds,
"I warn you—I'm the pirate chief, I am!"

Big black monster, sly and cunning,
gets the frightened pirates running.

But racing faster is the beast...

he only wants to share the feast!

Pirates noticing it's dark.   Pirates rushing through the park.

Pirates can't believe their eyes.

Up the gangplank,
then...

SURPRISE!
Scurvy scoundrels have a party,
playing games and laughing hearty.

To the ARRR-some gang I work with:
Betsy, Bridget, Jennifer, Karen, Pam, Paul, and Tomoko—LK

To my dad, who did sail the Seven Seas—JM

Library of Congress Cataloging-in-Publication
data is on file with the publisher.

Text copyright © 2015 by Leslie Kimmelman
Pictures copyright © 2015 by Albert Whitman & Company
Pictures by Jorge Monlongo
Published in 2015 by Albert Whitman & Company
ISBN 978-0-8075-8061-5

Printed in China
10 9 8 7 6 5 4 3 2 1 HH 20 19 18 17 16 15

Design by Jordan Kost

For more information about Albert Whitman & Company,
visit our web site at www.albertwhitman.com.